THE
WINTER BEAR

RUTH CRAFT

Illustrated by Erik Blegvad

D1364329

A MARGARET K. MC ELDERRY BOOK

Atheneum 1975 New York

MAR 1976

JEFFERSONVILLE TOWNSHIP PUBLIC LIBRARY
JEFFERSONVILLE, INDIANA

ं-e
C88856W

761796C

"Where's my boot?"
"Where's my sweater?"
"Where's my shoe?"
"I don't need a hat."
"Oh, yes you do!"
What a to-do!
You'd think it was a shipwreck,
But as you know,
When you walk in the winter,
Wherever you go,
You must put something on!

So, three set off
In the cold still air
With an apple or two,
(And plenty to wear).
And one jumped high.
And one jumped low.
And one walked backwards . . .
As far as he could go.

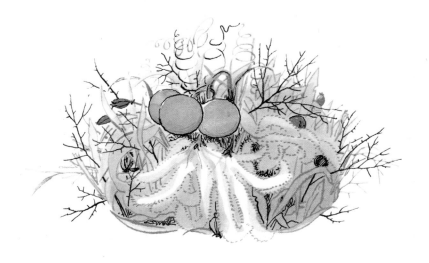

One gathered together a jaunty bouquet.
A bouquet? On a bleak winter's day?
But look . . . seeds, dried weeds,
Bryony vine and old man's beard.

One counted hungry birds.
How many could he see?
Birds in winter take what they can find –
Berries, husks, seeds and rinds,
All the pickings the year leaves behind.

One stroked a rough back.
"How now
Brown cow."
(Even a cow wears a sensible
winter coat just now.)

Three came to a hedge.
Two said, "Oh come on –
there's nothing there!"
But one stopped to stare . . .
Not at the bottom,
Not at the middle
But at the top.
Was that a sock?
Or a shoe?
Or what?

Take a stick . . . quick!
Carefully . . . mind!
Oh! What a find!
A brown knitted bear,

Knitted with care.
A bit damp, a bit leafy,
In need of repair,
But still, an excellent bear.

Hey!
Two came back.
"What have you there?"
"Good heavens! A bear!"

So four ran home
(That's three – and the bear),
Crying "Mum! Mum!
Here's a bear
In the winter with nothing to wear,
He must have something on!"

Two found some oddments
they thought would do.
One dried him off with a tissue or two.
And together they dressed him
And set him with care
On a round, brown cushion
In the best arm chair.

A warm friendly place
For a cold winter bear.

Text copyright © 1974 by Ruth Craft
Illustrations copyright © 1974 by Eric Blegvad
All rights reserved
Library of Congress catalog card number 74-18178
ISBN 0-689-50017-3. First American Edition